DAVE
Pigeon
(Racer!)

Dave Pigeon's Book on How to Beat a Dastardly Parrot

Typed up by Skipper
because **Swapna Haddow**
was busy making a cup of tea

Illustrated by
Sheena Dempsey
because she's better at
drawing maps than a pigeon

FABER & FABER

First published in 2018
by Faber and Faber Limited
Bloomsbury House
74–77 Great Russell Street
London WC1B 3DA

Designed by Faber and Faber
Printed and bound in the UK by
CPI Group (UK) Ltd, Croydon, CR0 4YY

Text © Swapna Haddow, 2018
Illustrations © Sheena Dempsey, 2018

A CIP record for this book is available from the British Library

ISBN/978-0-571-33690-6

2 4 6 8 10 9 7 5 3 1

For Felicity, a wonderful
Human Lady and a pigeontastic agent

SH and SD

Team Pawsville vets

Dave Pigeon

Skipper

Jet

Team Dazzle vets

Opprobrious Vastanavius
the Parrot

Mickey Lightning

Hello! I'm Skipper and that's my best friend, Dave Pigeon.
Good morning, good afternoon, good evening or good midnight snacking to you, you brilliant pigeon who chose to read my book and not that book over there. Or that book behind you. Or that book holding the door open.
As this is our third book, here's what you might've missed so far.
In our first book, Dave Pigeon, I lost my left wing in a savage attack by Mean Cat . . .
And a kind Human Lady took us in and gave us our very own home in her shed with a typewriter so we could write up all our stories.

1
The Three-Legged Dog in the Window

Have you ever sat in a shoebox? Of course you have.

But have you ever sat in one when your best friend Dave has spread himself out so wide that his cheesy feet are right up your beak and there also happens to be an old banana in the corner taking up the rest of the space?

I didn't think so.

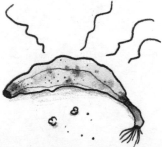

This is where our story begins. Our Human Lady had taken us away from our home in her shed earlier that evening and put Dave and me in a shoebox, on the front of her bike. There we were, rattling around in her bike basket as she cycled, wondering where we were going. The one good thing about Dave's cheesy claws was that they were covered in crispy crumbs from when he stepped in a pile of cheese puffs. Every time our Human Lady rode her bike over a bump, our shoebox rattled in her basket and stale crumbs fell in my mouth. Yum.

When the Human Lady eventually stopped cycling and Dave pulled back his feet, I managed to shuffle around and perch on the mouldy banana. Looking through a hole in the shoebox I could see we had stopped outside a shop. The walls were painted white with the words 'Pawsville Vets' printed on a dog-bone sign.

That's when I noticed a brown and white three-legged dog jumping about in the window.

And that's when I knew we were heading straight for trouble with an evil, lying parrot.

We'd not even met the parrot yet, Dave. Besides, it's a little early in the story to talk about that catbrained featherball . . .

Our Human Lady lifted us off her bike and took us into the shop. The door jingled as a bell above our head announced our arrival.

'What is this place?' Dave cooed.

I had no idea. The room was filled with squeaky toys and smelt of freshly washed dog fur. There were cosy pet beds and colourful dog leads piled on shelves and the painted murals of birds playing together made me smile.

'This is Dave and this is his friend, Skipper,' the Human Lady said, placing us on a countertop. I sat up in the box and looked around. A Human Man in a white coat was talking to our Human Lady. The three-legged dog from the window was now standing beside our Human Lady, sniffing her shoe, the same way I did when I wanted a sardine and salty crisp sandwich. Or I had an itchy bottom.

That's when a hamster in a ball rolled across the shelf above us, because that's what hamsters do, when they aren't busy getting stuck in sock drawers or toilets. There was a door where the shelf ended, and through the clear glass panels I could see a doctor's table surrounded by pet hutches and food bowls.

'Where are we?' Dave asked as we hopped out of the box on to the white worktop.

'You're at the vet's,' a voice said.

I turned to look down and the three-legged dog stared up at me with warm brown eyes. 'Welcome to Pawsville Vets,' she said. Her tail wagged and her eyes were bright and kind as she grinned at us.

'You speak Pigeonese?' I said.

'And Dog, Hamster and Goldfish,' she said, nodding proudly. 'I'm Jet, by the way.'

'I'm Skipper,' I said, waving my wing at her. 'And this is Dave.'

I reached over to introduce my friend but he was no longer next to me.

'Looks like Dave is getting his wing fixed,' Jet said, hobbling closer.

Dave lay still in our Human Lady's hands as she gently stroked his head while the Human Man in a white coat looked at the wing that Mean Cat had destroyed. The man then pulled over a small box and flipped up the lid. He gently peeled away the tissue paper inside and reached in.

The Human Man had built Dave a brand-new wing.

I pattered closer. The wing now lay on the countertop. Close up I could see dark grey feathers had been sewn together to form a wing shape. At the top was a brown leather harness, made of two loops that were strapped to the feathers.

'This is a prosthetic wing made from feathers I found in the park,' the Human Man told our Human Lady, pointing at the wing. 'It's the first one I've ever made.'

She gasped. 'Will Dave be able to fly again?'

'He will,' the man said with a smile.

I turned to Dave, whose beak hung open in awe. 'A new wing, Skipper,' he cooed. 'I'm getting a brand-new wing.'

The Human Lady set Dave down as the

Human Man unravelled Dave's sling. He threaded Dave's broken wing through the harness and pulled on the leather loops so that the new wing sat on top of his damaged left one.

Dave arched his back and pushed out both his wings. The prosthetic wing clicked and fanned out as though it was Dave's original wing all along.

'It's the most pigeontastic wing I've ever seen,' Dave squawked with glee. 'Let's see if I can fly.'

As he flapped his wings to take off, his feet lifted into the air. My friend was flying! I watched as he rose higher and higher while the new wing clicked and whooshed like a pair of bellows.

Before Dave could swoop any higher, the Human Man caught him in his hands and placed him back down by our Human Lady.

'You'll have to take it easy, little chap,' the man said to Dave.

'But he was flying,' the Human Lady said, grinning down at Dave and me. She dabbed at the happy tears in her eyes and her cheeks glowed a rosy red.

'Dave will have to rest here for a few days as he gets used to his new feathers,' the Human Man said whilst removing the new wing and slipping Dave's sling back on. 'If he flies too soon, he could tire himself out.'

'Did you hear that, Dave? No flying for you just yet,' the Human Lady said, kissing the top of Dave's head. 'Could Skipper stay with him?'

'Of course,' the man said, holding out a palm full of birdseed for me. He patted the feathers on my head as I pecked at the feed. 'I'll set up a little home for them out the back.'

'We have guests!' Jet barked, running around in circles. 'This is how all brilliant stories start.'

Dave hopped over to us as the Humans talked to each other. 'How do you know Pigeonese?' he asked Jet, his eyes narrowing.

'Well,' said Jet, leaning up close and brushing her wet nose against Dave's sling. 'It's because I ate the last pigeon who came to stay and now he speaks from inside me.'

2
The Worst Pirate Shanty in the World

Dave screeched as Jet licked her lips.

'I'm joking,' she said, yapping with laughter and going back to running around in circles. 'I'm the jokester around here.'

I wasn't screeching.

Yes, you were.

I was just practising my loudest coo.

Also known as screeching in terror.

'It's true,' the orange hamster said, rolling towards us. 'Jet makes jokes all the time. They're terrible but you'll get used to them.'

'You speak Pigeonese too?' I said to the hamster.

I was impressed. It wasn't every day you met a hamster who could do more than run in a big wheel.

I knew a hamster once.

Could he do more than run in a big wheel?

Yes.

What did he do?

He could also run in a medium-sized wheel.

15

'Jet taught me Pigeonese. She teaches all the pets,' the hamster squeaked. 'She's been here for years, ever since her owner abandoned her after she lost her leg. Now she can speak all the animal languages.'

Watching Jet scamper over the polished floor as she happily ran in circles, I wondered who would be so cruel as to give up such a cheerful dog. Maybe our Human Lady might be tempted to trade in her miserable Mean Cat for Jet?

'It's nice to meet you, Skipper,' the hamster said. 'I'm Gary.'

'And I'm Dave Pigeon,' Dave said, clicking out his

brand new wing and doing his loud 'I'm in charge around here' voice as he tried to cover up for his earlier screeching.

I wasn't screeching! I demand you remove that from the book, Skipper.

It's too late now, Dave. Everyone's read it.

There was absolutely no screeching, readers. Forget what Skipper just wrote.

Dave straightened up his feathers and turned to Jet. 'Does anyone know where the biscuits are?'

'We have to wait until the Vet Man leaves,' Jet said, nodding towards the man in the white coat. 'Then we raid the fridge and the cupboards in his kitchen.'

'What's a Vet Man?' I asked.

'He's a doctor who fixes sick and broken animals, like he just fixed your friend's wing,' Jet replied. 'I came here when I lost my leg.'

'And I'm here because I kept escaping from my cage and drinking water out of the Human toilets,' Gary piped up. 'I've survived three toilet flushings.'

The doorbell chimed again as our Human Lady waved us goodbye and left. I watched through the window as she rode off on her bike. I was glad Dave had got a new wing but I missed her already.

The Vet Man bundled up both Dave and me in his warm hands and carried us through to a back room. He reminded me of the Human Lady but smelt less of baked bread and more of toffee mints and stale socks.

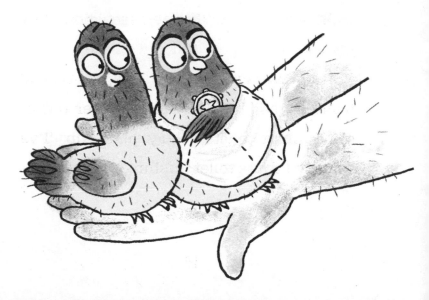

'That's Fluffle,' Jet yapped as she hopped along beside us, pointing to a cage with an iguana inside. 'She hurt her eye when she climbed into the back of her owner's television because she wanted to be on TV.'

'My favourite programme is *Pets Do the Dumbest Things*,' Fluffle said, her pink tongue flicking in and out as she spoke. 'Those animals are as daft as a reptile in a sweater.'

We were taken through to the back of the vet's, past more hutches and pet beds.

There were shelves with bottles and trays and Gary said these were medicines that helped make sick animals better.

'That's Cricket-Ball Face,' Gary squeaked, as he rolled after Jet.

We looked up to see a rabbit with a slightly squished face who was wiggling his nose at us. Jet barked up at him and Cricket-Ball Face hopped forward excitedly. Gary told us that the rabbit had accidentally hopped into a speeding Cricket-Ball and now he couldn't remember much, so Jet had named him Cricket-Ball Face.

The vet's was warm and bright and full of plump cushions and pet baskets. Of course, I loved living in the Human Lady's shed but I have to admit, it did get feather-freezingly cold during the winter. At night, I'd have to snuggle up close to Dave and he always snored and farted. Sometimes he did both at the same time. Here at Pawsville Vets, it looked like I could get a cosy bed lined with fluffy fleece all to myself.

'This place will do,' Dave announced with a nod, as the Vet Man set us down inside a birdhouse that was filled with soft golden sawdust.

'Do you think you will be staying long?' Gary asked, spinning towards us in his ball.

'I don't think so,' Dave said. 'We have

our own shed. It's about a thousand and six times the size of this birdhouse.' He nodded at the little gated cage. 'We even have our own supply of bread and biscuits.' He puffed out his chest feathers as the animals ooohed in awe.

'Have a good sleep, animals,' the Vet Man called out, as he locked the back door and waved us goodbye.

We all said 'Good night' back to him but he didn't respond because he didn't speak Pigeonese, Dog, Hamster, Iguana or slightly squished Rabbit.

Of course, we had no intention of going to sleep. I was keen to explore and Dave was keen to find biscuits. As soon as the Vet Man left, Dave slipped off his sling and began struggling with the harness of his new wing.

'The Vet Man said you have to rest,' I reminded Dave.

'I'm a pigeon,' Dave said. 'Who would you trust when it comes to wings? A Human or a bird?'

'But—'

'Stop butting and help me with this strap.'

I sighed, then grabbed the two loops of leather in my beak and wriggled them up over Dave's wing, just like the Vet Man had done. It clicked into place and Dave batted me away as he spread out his new feathers.

'Ta-daaaa—' Dave started.

DONK!

'I said "ta-daaaa—"'

DONK! DONK! DONK!

Large dark shadows fell over our cage as something crashed into the window.

'What's that?' Dave squawked. 'I'm in the middle of my "ta-daaaaah".'

DONK! DONK! DONK!

'Jet!' I shouted. 'Is everything OK?'

'It's the Dazzle birds,' Jet said. Her head was huddled down between her shoulders, as if she'd known to expect the sound of heavy bodies bashing against the glass. 'They've landed.'

DONK! DONK! DONK! DONK, DONK, DONK!

'Who are the Dazzle birds?'

'Opprobrious Vastanavius the Parrot and his crew,' Gary groaned, crawling out of his ball. 'They're from the super swanky vet's down the road, called Dazzle.'

Outside the window, a large scarlet macaw stood proud, with his head held high in the night air and his chest puffed out. He wore a black patch over one eye. As he peered through the glass, leering at us, two green and yellow budgerigars and a fluffy white cockatoo flew down to join him.

'If you ignore them, they'll go away,' Jet said.

'Can't we just ask them to keep the noise down?' I said, shouting over the scratchy cawing and whooping from the window.

'They make fun of us.'

'Why would they make fun of you?'

'They make fun of all the pets here at

Pawsville Vets. They come here every
night to laugh at us for not being as fancy
as them.'

The hoots of laughter from the window got louder and louder. The budgies linked wings and started to swing each other around, singing out a pirate shanty:

Braaaand new guests at Pawsville Vets,
A pauper's vet is what they gets.
Opprobrious and his shipmate crew,
From Dazzle we come, to laugh at you!

'They're pirates?' I asked Jet.

She nodded. 'Opprobrious Vastanavius the Parrot is a retired pirate parrot and that's his crew of birdy shipmates. They're always looking for a fight.'

The budgies continued to dance, spinning faster and faster as Opprobrious Vastanavius the Parrot tapped his foot to the beat of the shanty.

'Pirates or not, no one laughs at me for no reason,' Dave said.

He straightened up his new wing and walked over to the window.

'Hello, birdies and birdlemen,' Dave said. 'I'm Dave Pigeon.'

'Dave Pigeon from that book called Dave Pigeon?' the cockatoo squawked back.

'Yes,' Dave said, proudly.

'And the same Dave Pigeon from that other book called Dave Pigeon (Nuggets!)?' one of the budgerigars shrieked.

'That's me!' Dave said, turning to grin at me.

A gaggle of roars and howls from the birds on the other side of the window pierced the night air as they rolled about laughing on the ledge:

Dave's a pigeon and we know what that means,
He smells just like a tin of baked beans.
He's only one wing like a sack of apples
Because he sucks feathers and pineapples!

'What does that even mean?' Dave asked, confused. 'That's the worst shanty in the world.'

'Silence!' the parrot barked at his cronies. He eyeballed Dave with his one eye. 'It means I know all about you and I have no idea how you can even call yourself a bird.' He spat out the word 'bird' so hard that a glob of parrot spit landed on the glass.

I flew over to the window and landed next to Dave. He was mad. His feathers were huffy and fluffy and the grey in his face was turning a hot reddy-purple.

'You are an embarrassment, Dave Pigeon,' Opprobrious Vastanavius the Parrot continued. 'An embarrassment to all birdkind.'

'No, he's not,' I shouted. 'He's more bird than any smelly parrot could ever be.'

Opprobrious Vastanavius the Parrot spun to stare at me. 'And you must be the useless sidekick.'

Jet pounced at the window, scaring the birds up off the ledge. She growled, 'That's enough, Opprobrious Vastanavius the Parrot. Every night you land here and make jokes about our home but now you've gone too far, insulting our new guests.'

The parrot leaned up against the window and snarled at Dave. 'Not bird enough to fight your own battles, you need your scallywag dog to do it?' he taunted him.

Dave exploded, 'How dare you, you, you, you—'

Opprobrious Vastanavius the Parrot laughed as Dave struggled to find a good comeback.

'He can out-bird you any day,' I screeched.

'That's right, I can,' Dave squawked.

'Fine,' the cockatoo hooted. 'Let's put it to the test.'

'Anything you can do, I can do a gazillion times better,' Dave said.

'There's only one place to prove how much of a bird you are.' The parrot's beak curled up in a smirk. 'And that's on the high clouds of the seven skies.'

My throat went nine-crackers dry. Did I hear right? Was he challenging Dave to a race? The very same Dave who had never raced in his life?

'How about it, pigeon?' Opprobrious Vastanavius the Parrot goaded. 'Can you beat me in a race?'

'A race? You want to take me on in a race?' Dave squawked with laughter. 'You do know pigeons were born to race.' He flicked out his new wing to show off to the rival birds.

'We'll see about that, you scurvy pigeon,' Opprobrious Vastanavius the Parrot smirked, his beak curling up on one side.

'Hang on, Dave,' I whispered to my friend. 'Remember the Vet Man said you needed to rest.'

'Don't be silly, Skipper. This wing doesn't need rest. It needs to fly,' Dave crowed. 'And that parrot needs to be put in his place.'

My heart sank to my claws. 'I really don't think this is a good idea—'

Dave shushed me while the parrot laughed in his face. We were already in too deep. Opprobrious Vastanavius the Parrot and his shipmates would never leave us alone if Dave pulled out now.

'In three days' time, we race!' Opprobrious Vastanavius the Parrot declared. 'And if I win, you have to admit parrots are better than pigeons.'

'And if I win, you have to admit parrots are a waste of feathers and you and your crew must promise never to return to Pawsville Vets for the rest of your life,' Dave replied.

'Deal.'

'Deal.'

'I said "deal" first.'

'I said it second.'

'Deal with it.'

'I've dealt with it.'

'Whoever smelt it, dealt it.'

'Deal the cards.'

'Huh?' the parrot said. 'It's a deal.'

'Good riddance to bad feathers,' Dave said, as he watched the Dazzle crew swoop up into the dark. And then he shouted 'Deal!' at the fleeing birds to make sure he had the last squawk. My stomach felt like a knot of nesty twigs in a washing machine. I couldn't shake the feeling Dave was doomed.

'The last time a pigeon said "deal",' Jet whispered to me, 'he ended up in a sandwich.'

3
The True History of Racer Pigeons According to Dave Pigeon

'I'm joking!' Jet said, seeing my horrified face.

Jet's jokes really are terrible.

We don't have time for her awful jokes, Skipper.

You're right, Dave. I'll give her a page right at the end of the book.

39

But it wasn't Jet's joke that had me scared.

I'd known Dave since we were squabs. He'd never been the fastest pigeon in the park. And he had two wings back then. Somebody had to tell him this was an impossible feat.

I turned to my best friend. 'There is no way you can beat that parrot. You've never raced before.'

'Don't worry, Skipper. I have racing pigeon in my DNA,' Dave said. 'No other bird can beat a racing pigeon. We're the fastest birds on the planet.'

'I thought the peregrine falcon was the fastest bird,' Jet said.

'Pah,' Dave scoffed. 'Falcons are just big pigeons.'

41

Oh yes. Sorry. The Pigeonasaurus was gallant and grey and was the fastest-flying dinosaur known to dinosaurkind.
I thought the first-ever pigeon was the Archaeopteryx.
Also known as the Pigeonasaurus.
Over millions of years, pigeons proved that they could not be beaten.
Our speed was well known and we were legendary for our super-fast message delivery service.
The fastest pigeon ever recorded flew at more than 100 miles an hour!

'And that's why I know I will win this race,' Dave chirped to Jet and me with his proudest pigeon nod.

'This is never going to work,' Jet said under her dog breath, as we watched Dave admire his new wing. 'And that's not a joke.'

4

Jet's Worst Plan

The next day, I knew I had to be positive. Dave was up against the meanest parrot I'd ever met and there was no way to back out. And it looked like Jet and Gary thought the same thing.

We were woken up by the Vet Man, who arrived early in the morning to top up our food bowls. All apart from Dave, who was dozing in his sawdust bed, hugging his new wing close.

The Human left soon after and Jet hurried over to Dave, waking him up with

her wet nose. 'Morning, Dave,' she barked.
'I have a plan.'

'And I have breakfast,' Gary said,
pushing a plate towards us.

It was piled high with
bread and biscuits,
including my favourite
jammy ones.

'Where did you get all
these goodies?' I said,
pecking at a gooey centre.

'We ransacked the Human's kitchen,' Gary said.

'Delicious,' Dave said, as jam dripped from his feathers on to his good wing. 'What's the plan, Jet?'

'We are going to spy on Opprobrious Vastanavius the Parrot and his crew at Dazzle and see what they are up to. That way we'll know what we are up against.'

'That's a brilliant idea,' Gary said, gnawing at a carrot. 'If I know that dastardly parrot, he will definitely be training for the race already.'

This was a bad idea. If the pirate crew caught us spying on them, we would all be feather-deep in trouble.

But Jet was about to spring an even

worse idea on us.

My guts were churning like a ball of ice cream in a glass of fizzy pop but I managed to eat half a biscuit before Jet suggested it was time we started off to Dazzle.

'What about the Vet Man?' I asked Jet, remembering Humans liked to turn up to work so they could play computer games and drink tea. 'Won't he notice we're gone?'

'Don't be a worrying whippet, Skipper,' she replied. 'I checked his calendar and it's his weekend off. He won't be back until Monday.'

She led us to a large cupboard by the side of the main waiting area. 'We'll need camouflage so we don't stand out amongst the Humans,' she said. 'We can find the perfect disguise in the lost property room.'

The room was stashed full of coats and scarves and unpaired gloves and abandoned dog leads. Dave headed for a discarded handbag and poked around the pockets for old biscuits and bread crusts.

After all, everyone knows that's what handbags are for.

'Follow me.' Jet grinned.

She grabbed hold of an old blanket that lay over a mystery object the size and shape of a bike, only wider. 'Help me,' she said, as she pulled at the cloth with her mouth.

Me and Dave hopped over and tugged and grabbed at the blanket. Something was pinning it down. I flew up over the top and pulled it with my feet as I flapped up hard. The blanket gave way and flowed down to the floor, covering Dave.

'What is that?' Dave asked, as he came up through the folds of the blanket.

'That, my feathered friends, is my plan.' Jet beamed a toothy smile.

The blanket had fallen to reveal a shiny red motorised scooter. Not the ones Little Humans ride the pavements on. No, this was a scooter with a seat, complete with shopping basket on the front, an engine and fat-tyred wheels.

While me and Dave admired the vehicle, Jet grabbed a bright purple coat that had once belonged to a Little Human. She put her paw through one sleeve and the other sleeve dangled by her side. Then she picked up a dusty baby blanket and joined us by the scooter.

'Somebody left their scooter here?' I said in awe.

'Yup,' Jet said. 'You'd be surprised what people forget at the vet's. One time

a Human Man forgot his Christmas tree!'

She licked a bit of dirt off the front panel of the scooter and shined the bumper with her snout.

'I'll sit in the seat,' she said, explaining her idea. 'And I'll put the blanket over my legs. You two can use the controls to steer us over to Dazzle.'

Jet wanted us to drive the scooter over to Dazzle.

This was the worst plan I'd ever heard.

And that included all of Dave's catbrained ideas.

Skipper! My ideas are brilliant.

What about that time you thought we should try and post ourselves to the beach to get a free holiday?

I still think that's a pigeontastic idea. We just need to find an envelope big enough.

'You think we can drive this thing?' I asked Jet.

'Yes!'

'Even if we could drive the scooter,' I said, not quite believing we were having this conversation, 'don't you think a dog and two pigeons driving a motorised scooter will somehow stand out more to the Humans than if we just walked over to Dazzle?'

'Of course not!' Jet exclaimed. 'The Humans will think I'm a Human because I'll be wearing a Human coat.'

I looked over at Dave for support. If anyone was going to find this idea as mad as I did, it would be him.

'Jet, I'm not sure this is a great idea—' he started.

I nodded along, thankful one of them could see sense.

'I think it might be the GREATEST idea I've ever heard in my whole life,' Dave said. 'I can't believe I didn't come up with it myself!'

'What?'

'Come on, Skipper,' Dave said. 'Stop being such a negative nightingale.'

I sighed, watching Dave and Jet egg each other on. Outnumbered, there was no way to convince them this would never work.

'How do we even turn it on?'

'Like this,' Dave said, hopping up on to the scooter and clambering up to the controls. He twisted a key jangling in the handlebar with his beak and the scooter roared to life. 'Climb on,' he yelled at Jet over the noise.

'Are you coming?' Jet asked. 'We need your help.'

I looked at the dog in her purple coat and my best friend sitting on the handlebars. Dave's eyes twinkled with excitement. This was a terrible idea but I couldn't let him down.

I flew up on to the scooter and sat next to Dave as he and Jet squealed with delight. As Dave jumped across to make space for me, he whacked the handlebar with his bottom. The scooter spun out of the storeroom, across the polished floor of the waiting room and straight towards a bin. Dave and me screeched as Jet howled for help. We skidded out of control, whacking

a table and driving over a magazine rack before the scooter finally crashed into the reception desk, refusing to move.

Jet leapt off the scooter as it purred and the engine died. 'I'm very surprised that didn't work,' she barked. 'We'll just have to walk to Dazzle.'

'I agree,' Dave said, hopping off the scooter.

'I said that we should walk from the beginning—' I told them.

'Skipper, we don't have time for one of your "I told you sos",' Dave squawked, cutting me off.

I still can't believe that plan didn't work.

You can't believe that a dog and two pigeons couldn't drive a Human scooter?

Maybe it's because we forgot to put raspberry jam in the engine.

You don't put jam in the engine, Dave!

Of course you do. And because we didn't put any in the scooter, that's why it crashed.

Jet woofed loudly for Gary to join us as she pounced behind the reception desk. She stood up on her hind legs and reached with her one front paw for the keys under the worktop. Passing the heavy hoop of jangling metal carefully from her paw to her mouth, she scampered out from behind the desk, her claws clattering on the floor. Her head bobbed towards the front door, signalling us to hurry ahead of her.

The lock to the door was a little higher than the desk and I wondered how we would get the key in. I followed Jet's gaze to Gary, who had been rolling himself back.

Suddenly, a flash of plastic and orange fur blasted past me as Gary scampered hard towards the door. His ball spun and then halted as his back paws shot out of two holes in the plastic and he grabbed the doormat.

Dave and me watched open-beaked as Jet ran at the

door and jumped, landing on Gary's ball on her hind legs, like a circus performer. She stretched and reached high to unlock the door with the key clasped in her paw.

'Let's go,' Jet said, climbing down from Gary's ball and opening the door.

'Wow,' I said. 'How did you learn to do that?'

'It didn't go well the first few times,' Gary said, rolling after me. 'One time, Jet landed the wrong way up and I was bowled right across the vet's, through the dog flap and out of the back door.'

'Why didn't we just use the dog flap to get outside?'

Both Jet and Gary stood silent, staring

at each other. After a moment Gary broke the silence.

'That's actually a good idea,' he said.

After Gary waved us off, Jet barked and yapped all the way to Dazzle. Dave was keen to try out his new wing, so we flew ahead of Jet as she bounded off to the rival vet's, her ears pricked and tail wagging. Dave grew tired quickly as he wasn't used to the weight of his wing, so when we spotted a Little Human being pulled along on her roller skates we hitched a ride by perching on Jet's back while she hung on to the folds of the Little Human's long princess dress.

A large white building with grand

windows appeared soon enough and Jet told us this was where we needed to get off. We'd made it to Dazzle.

As we ran up to the fancy vet's a huge glass door slid open. We didn't have to push it and wait for the bell to tinkle above our heads like we did at Pawsville.

I could see why it was called Dazzle. The whole place was bright white from the walls to the floors to the ceiling. There were white padded thrones in the waiting areas and a waterfall wall behind the reception desk. Humans hurried around, taking their pets for manicures and massages, and didn't notice us at all as we crept towards the back of the room.

'Look at this place,' Dave exclaimed.

Spa

Pawdicures

It was hard not to be dazzled at Dazzle. My feathers already felt fancier for being there.

'I don't see what the big deal is,' Jet grumbled.

'Have you seen the food bowls?' Dave continued. 'They're encrusted with jewels!'

A hairless chihuahua drinking from a nearby bowl looked up at us for a moment. She tossed her head in disgust as she eyed up Jet's three legs and Dave's one wing. Then she went back to sipping her diamond water.

And there it was. The reason no one at Pawsville

liked Dazzle. Gary was right. These animals thought they were better than everyone else and they hadn't even given us a chance.

'Let's go before we're spotted,' I said, hurrying Dave along as he continued to gawp at the opulence. I was starting to feel like my feathers were out of place among the posh pets at Dazzle.

Jet's plan was to find Opprobrious Vastanavius the Parrot and spy on him and his crew. She and Gary were convinced the parrot would be up to no good and we needed to know what that was.

We headed through the fancy foyer and followed Jet up a spiral staircase. 'I can hear Opprobrious Vastanavius the Parrot and his friends,' she growled in a whisper.

As we turned the corner at the top of the stairs the sounds of squawks and parrot shanties grew louder. We carried on across the landing and found ourselves in a small hallway facing the glass door of a studio.

'They're in there,' Jet murmured.

Careful not to trigger the sliding door, we snuck up as close as we could and peered in through the glass.

Opprobrious Vastanavius the Parrot was jumping up and down as one of his cronies yelled instructions to go 'higher' and 'faster'.

'Looks like they have a professional coach training Opprobrious Vastanavius the Parrot,' Dave said.

There was something very familiar about the coach's voice. Something I couldn't quite put my finger on. I twisted to get a better view and made out the shape of a medium-sized bird. A shape I knew well. Too well.

The shape of a pigeon.

'Isn't that the world-famous, legendary racing pigeon, Mickey Lightning?' Jet whispered, squinting through the glass.

I looked hard and recognised the pigeon right in front of us.

Jet was right. It was Mickey Lightning.

Dave's face fell as he recognised him too.

'Why's your dad training Opprobrious Vastanavius the Parrot?' I said.

5
The Legend of Mickey Lightning

Dave's dad, aka Mickey Lightning, was nothing like I remembered. When we were younger, just little squabs hunting around under park benches for croissants, we would watch his dad train for races. His chest would ripple as the muscles under his feathers stretched, pushing him forward as he rocketed up into the sky at the speed of lightning.

Now, as Mickey stepped into view, I could see the feathers around his chest were stumpy and straggly with age. His voice was gruff, like sandpaper. And he'd started to lose the feathers on his crown.

But the pigeon standing in the studio was definitely Dave's father.

'Mickey Lightning is your dad?' Jet barked.

The grey in Dave's face faded as he pressed closer to the glass to watch his dad stretch out the parrot's scarlet wings. He paled from grey pigeon, to not so grey pigeon, to even less grey pigeon, all the way to white dove, as we listened to Mickey and Opprobrious Vastanavius the Parrot break into a fit of giggly screeches over a joke about a chicken and a duck.

'Dad?' Dave whispered, his eyes wide in disbelief.

As he pushed closer, his new wing clicked and snapped out, whacking the glass door so that it shot open. Both Dave and Jet bowled into the studio, all feathers and paws.

For a moment there was silence as we stared at Dave's dad and he stared right back at us.

'What are you scurvy lot doing here?'

Opprobrious Vastanavius the Parrot squawked just as Jet started yowling hysterically. I tried to pull Dave back as the parrot's shipmate crew howled and shrieked, crashing towards us, trying to push us out of the room.

Mickey stood still, unmoving.

I grabbed Dave by the wing as he continued to stare at his dad. 'Let's go!'

'Are you OK?' I asked Dave.

He'd been chirping away about the best ingredients for a good macaroni and strawberry trifle all the way back to the safety of Pawsville.

'Of course I'm fine, Skipper,' Dave squawked, his feathers all huffy and fluffy, which meant he was anything but fine. 'I'm the finest I've ever been. Finey, finey, finey fine.'

He pecked at the harness of his new wing to slide it off. His beak got trapped under the leather strap and as I went to help, he pulled away hard, pinging it in his face. 'I need to rest, Skipper,' he said, nuzzling his bruised beak in his good wing. 'The key to winning a race is staying as still as possible, don't you know?'

He slunk towards the back of the vet's. Me and Jet waited in the reception area, by the abandoned scooter. We heard the clang of Dave's cage where I knew he'd crumpled into his sawdust bed.

'What's going on?' Jet whispered. 'Why

won't Dave talk about his dad?'

We settled on a worn dog bed by the window and drank water from a dog bowl. It would be down to me to tell Jet about my friend and his father.

'Dave adored his dad,' I started. 'They were inseparable.'

I told Jet about how we used to help Mickey train, how we would pretend to race him and how he would let us win.

'As word spread about Mickey's talent, he hit the big time. Humans were paying lots of money to see him race and Mickey chose the life of a racer pigeon over living at home with Dave and the family.' I sighed. 'One of the last things he told Dave was to go and find his own path. He promised to stay in touch. But that never happened. Mickey and Dave grew apart and the last time Dave saw his father was four Pigeon years ago . . . until just now at Dazzle.'

'Blimey-salami!' Jet said. 'No wonder Dave is upset.'

A knock at the window interrupted Jet. The door swung open a small bit, enough for the bell to ring.

It was Mickey.

'What is he doing here?' Jet yelped.

Mickey bowed to Jet and swooped over to me, picking me up in a feathery hug.

'Hello, Mickey,' I said awkwardly. Old feelings came flooding back as his familiar scent of a crisp winter's day and freshly cut grass came wafting up my nostrils. In that moment it would've been easy to forget that he'd let Dave down.

But I didn't forget.

I stepped back from Mickey and noticed how much he and Dave looked alike now. The balding heads and stumpy necks. There was no doubting they were father and son.

'Where is he?' Mickey asked, looking around.

'I think Dave wants to be left alone,' Jet said.

'The dog speaks Pigeonese?' Mickey said to me.

'Her name is Jet and she's our friend,' I said defensively.

'All right, all right!' Mickey said, holding up his wings. 'Keep your plumey knickers on!'

We stood staring at each other for a moment.

'He goes by the name "Dave"?' Mickey asked, breaking the silence.

'We have a Human Lady now,' I explained. 'She named us. She calls me Skipper.'

'A Human Lady, eh?' Mickey looked impressed. 'Does that mean a constant supply of bread and biscuits—'

'Dad?'

We all spun around to find Dave watching us.

'Son!'

Mickey swooped over and wrapped his wings around Dave. 'How are you, my boy?'

'Completely fine,' Dave said, pulling away from his dad. 'Feather-flumpingly fine actually. Finey, finey, finey fine, if you must know.'

Jet nudged me and I could see she was thinking what I was thinking. This was a private moment and we shouldn't be here.

But Dave held up a wing to stop us as we went to leave the room. 'Where have you been all this time, Dad?'

Mickey fell silent. He looked down and mumbled into his chest feathers. 'I wish I could tell you but you wouldn't understand.'

'What wouldn't we understand?' I asked.

'It's hard to explain,' Mickey cooed. 'But you know the racing world. It's busy . . . and with all the travelling, I just couldn't keep in contact.'

He reached up to put a wing on Dave's shoulder but Dave shrugged him off.

'You could've sent a carrier pigeon,' Dave huffed.

'You did promise to stay in touch,' I said, folding my wings in front of my chest. 'If you aren't going to tell us what happened, you should just go.'

'OK, OK,' Mickey squawked. He took a

breath and gulped. 'The truth is I got lost.'

Jet's jaw almost hit the floor. "The great Mickey Lightning got lost?'

The feathers around Mickey's face darkened with a bluish blush as the enormity of what he was saying sank in. Pigeons like Mickey didn't get lost. They just didn't. That's the special thing about us homing pigeons. We always find our way home to our nests.

'It's my most shameful secret,' Mickey whispered.

'I don't understand, Dad,' Dave cawed. 'What happened?'

We sat down around Mickey as he told us the story of his last training session before a big race. I remembered Dave and me had waved him off that morning as he lunged from the family nest and soared through the blue sky to his Racing Human Owner.

'I was being coached to win my final race,' Mickey cried. 'And then I was going to retire.'

Mickey's Human Owner had released him as he always did when they trained. As he flew higher and higher he'd started to tire and he came down and settled in a garden for a pit stop.

'That's when my troubles

started,' Mickey said. 'I zoomed back up to find my way home and suddenly I wasn't sure of where I was at all. It was like my pigeon instincts had left me completely and I had no idea why.'

Mickey kept going though. Every time he panicked he turned right.

'I just kept flying and flying, hoping I'd find my way home.'

He followed his beak, turning right after right after right, trailing the curve of the planet all the way around, until four pigeon years later he'd made his way back.

'You flew around the entire world in six Human months?' I exclaimed.

Mickey nodded. 'Oh, the things I've seen, my feathered friend. I flew with the wild flying fish of the Caribbean, drank fresh spicy tea from the chaiwalas in India, soared across the snow-capped mountains of the Alps and shook my tail feathers alongside the carnival floats in Rio.'

Mickey's eyes glazed over as he remembered the glorious sights of his travels. 'I've only just arrived back,' he twittered on. 'I ran into

Opprobrious Vastanavius the Parrot and his friends at Dazzle after a kind Human found me, tired and cold, and took me in for a check-up.'

Mickey turned to Dave and held out his wings for a hug. 'Do you see now that I never meant to abandon you? Can you forgive me, son?'

Dave looked away. 'I s'pose.'

'Do I see a smile?' Mickey teased, edging closer to Dave. 'Is that a smile from my pigeontastic boy?'

'Yes, I am pigeontastic,' Dave chirruped, reluctantly.

'Who's pigeontastic? You are! You are!' Mickey started singing. 'Come on, son, you do the next bit.'

It was the song he used to sing to us as squabs. 'I'm pigeontastic. Me am. Me am,' Dave twittered back.

Mickey's words were working. The song we'd danced around to as youngsters was bringing Dave out of his grumpiness. His dad hadn't abandoned him at all. He had been lost all this time and now he was back. Dave sang and stamped his feet as his father hugged him and they both called me over to join in.

'Who's pigeontastic? You are! You are!' Mickey and me warbled.

'I'm pigeontastic. Me am! Me am!' Dave sang back.

Sing it with me, Skipper!
Who's pigeontastic? You are! You are!
I'm pigeontastic. Me am. Me am.
I love this song.
Do you remember when I sang it so loud I scared off another pigeon and ate all the bread he left behind?
Yes. That was me. Yesterday. You screeched right down my earhole.
Oh. Yes. Sorry about that.

'Come on, Jet,' I said, nudging my three-legged friend. 'Join in.'

'This song is dumb,' she said, looking suspiciously at Mickey. '"Me am" doesn't even make sense.'

'Does someone not want to join in?' Mickey said, ribbing Jet as he and Dave pranced over to us.

'You haven't explained what you were doing with Opprobrious Vastanavius the Parrot,' Jet growled.

'I'm just training him,' Mickey said. 'He has a race against a pigeon . . .' His voice tailed off as he finally understood why we were there. 'Oh no, son,' he said, turning to Dave. 'Don't tell me you're the pigeon he's racing?'

'Yup,' Dave crowed proudly. 'I'm going to beat that vile Opprobrious Vastanavius the Parrot and show the world I'm a racing pigeon just like my dad.'

'And now, you know, it's time to pick a side,' Jet said. 'Are you Team Dazzle or Team Pawsville?'

'Obviously Dad is on my side,' Dave chirped. 'You always pick the winning side, don't you?'

'Of course, son,' Mickey said quietly.

'Told you!' Dave hugged Jet and they bounced up and down.

'This is dogtastic news. The actual racing legend Mickey Lightning is going to help us,' Jet howled. 'Welcome to Team Pawsville!'

As Jet and Dave celebrated, I watched

Mickey. Something was wrong. He could barely look Dave in the eye.

'Time for biscuits,' I announced, as Jet and my best friend skipped across the room. 'Why don't you get a feast out for us, Dave?'

'Good idea, Skipper!' Dave grinned. 'Dad's back and we have a lot to celebrate.'

That's reminded me. I think it's time for a biscuit.

Good idea. Have a look on the shelf. I think we have a stash of shortbread.

Now that Dave is gone, I'm going to tell you what happened next. But you have to Pigeon's Promise never to tell Dave what I'm about to reveal, OK?

Jet and Dave hopped to the kitchen, but I hung back.

'What's wrong, Mickey?' I asked, once I had him to myself. 'You'd better not be having second thoughts.'

'Of course not.' Mickey watched his son. 'It's not that.'

'What is it?'

Mickey hesitated. 'The thing is, Skipper, there is something I should have told him a long time ago.'

I began to fear what I was about to hear. 'What's wrong?'

Mickey's voice was grave. He stared
hard at the floor. 'Dave is not a racing
pigeon.'

6
The Truth About Dave Pigeon

'Of course he is!'

Mickey shook his head.

'But he's your son!'

'And that's exactly why he can't be a racing pigeon.' Mickey leaned in. He came up so close to my earhole I could feel his beak in my feathers. 'I'm not a racing pigeon.'

There was silence.

'Of course you are!' I burst out laughing, spitting over the floor. 'You're the legendary racing pigeon, Mickey Lightning.'

In a small voice, he said, 'I'm a utility pigeon. Just like Dave's mother. And just like Dave. We aren't racing pigeons. We're built to taste good.'

'A utility pigeon?' I said. 'I guess that would explain why cats like to eat Dave. But how on pigeon's earth did you manage to become the best racing pigeon known to pigeonkind?'

'I trained, son,' Mickey said. 'I wanted to be more than just a pigeon in a pie, so I trained for years and years until I was good enough.' He shrugged as if there was nothing to it.

I felt my heart plummet to my claws and right through the floor. 'We don't have years and years, Mickey! Dave is racing the day after tomorrow.'

'I know!'

'We have to tell him.'

'NO!' Mickey said, grabbing me. 'The only thing getting him through is that he thinks he is a racing pigeon.'

The idea of lying to Dave made me feel sick to my stomach. He was my best friend.

'His wing is badly damaged. He's got a new one but the Vet Man thinks he shouldn't be racing with it any time soon.'

'Since when did Humans know more about feathers than pigeons?' Mickey scoffed.

Dave and Mickey were starting to sound more alike than ever.

'I know this is hard,' Mickey continued.

'I will try my very best to get him into shape before the race but you know him. If we tell him this now he will give up before he even starts.'

'If we tell him, we can call off this silly race before he humiliates himself.'

Mickey shook his head. 'I know that parrot and he's vicious. He will destroy you all if you call off the race.'

'Are you two coming?' Jet yelped from the kitchen. 'Dave's found a stash of toffee biscuits and he's eating them all.'

'That's not true,' Dave hooted, poking his head out around the corner. His beak was covered in biscuit crumbs and goo. 'They're chocolate biscuits.'

'We're coming,' Mickey squawked back. He turned to me, grabbing my wings. 'Don't tell anyone the truth about Dave.'

Torn between wanting to protect my friend and not wanting to lie to him, I made a decision. 'Fine. But you'd better not let Dave down.'

'Pigeon's Promise,' Mickey said. 'Cross my heart, hope to die, stick a peanut in my eye.'

That night we feasted with Mickey, Jet, Gary, Fluffle the iguana and Cricket-Ball Face the rabbit. Gary was beside himself to be in the same room as the Mickey Lightning, let alone sharing dinner with him. Everyone laughed and danced and binged on biscuits and when darkness fell,

they all went to bed.
But I stayed up late,
unable to switch off
my brain. I couldn't
shake the feeling Dave
was heading beak first
into disaster.

'Mickey?' I whispered into the dark, over the sound of Dave's snores. 'Do you think Dave can do this?'

'Of course he can, Skipper.' Mickey yawned, turning over sleepily. 'If you really want to do something and you try hard enough, you can achieve it.'

7

Dave Versus Dave's Dad

Remember the big secret about Dave? He's going to be back at the end of this chapter, so keep those beaks sealed.

'UP UP UP!'

I woke to the shrieks of Mickey, bashing a spoon against our cage.

'Dad! It's too early!' Dave cried.

'The race is tomorrow, son,' Mickey cooed. 'We don't have much time.'

Jet growled as Mickey landed on her head and peeled an eyelid open with his claw. 'We need everyone up to help,' Mickey screeched.

Only Gary was raring to go as he spun around in his ball in excitement.

A sleepy Dave hopped out of bed and yawned as he joined his dad.

'You need to be awake and switched on, son,' Mickey squawked. 'Are you a pigeON or a pigeOFF?'

'A pigeon?'

'I'm a pigeon,' Gary shouted, rolling up

beside Dave.

'You're a hamster,' Mickey shouted back.
'Don't be a wally.'

Me and Jet lined up next to Gary and
Dave as Fluffle and Cricket-Ball Face joined
us. Mickey marched up and down the line,
inspecting us like an officer in the army.

'Today, we train,' he squawked.
'Tomorrow, we soar.'

He pointed at Gary. 'Do you have the jammy biscuits?'

'Yes, sir!'

He turned to Dave. 'Every time you do well, you get a biscuit.'

'That will be easy,' Dave scoffed. 'I'm a racing pigeon.'

I couldn't look Dave in the eye. 'What happens if he doesn't do well?' I asked, changing the subject.

'Then he will have to clean out the tiny poos in Cricket-Ball Face's hutch.'

'Yuck,' Dave said.

'And I warn you that Cricket-Ball Face had a double helping of rabbit pellets yesterday so his poo is a little runny.'

As everyone gathered around the

rabbit's hutch to see if what Mickey had said was true, Dave called me over to help him put his new wing on. He pecked off his sling and we slid the harness on. As I tugged the straps tight with my beak and the feathers clicked into place, Mickey whistled in awe.

'That's a wing of beauty, my boy,' he said to Dave.

'It is,' Dave said, fanning the feathers open. 'With my racing-pigeon blood and this wing, I won't need any training at all.'

Mickey and I exchanged awkward looks as Dave started pecking his way into the centre of a chocolate-orange biscuit. I wanted to tell my friend the horrible secret that was weighing my feathers down with guilt but I knew I couldn't. If Dave was going to stand any chance of beating Opprobrious Vastanavius the Parrot, he'd have to believe he was born to race.

'Follow me!' Mickey crowed at Dave.

He'd been busy. The reception area had been transformed into an assault course. There were hoops and squeaky toys on the floor and water bowls strung from the ceiling. Smelly hills of dog food dotted the floor and hamster-wheel towers were stacked high.

'What is this?' Dave asked.

'This is your training circuit, son,' Mickey said.

Seeing the doubt in his son's eyes, he called me over to show Dave what to do. Mickey set me to work, asking me to hurdle over the hoops and leap high up to the dog bowls. Once I'd done this, he made me circle higher and higher, until I was looping around the ceiling and the waiting-room floor looked like a blur. When I landed, I felt dizzy and I could feel breakfast-biscuit sick rising up through my throat and into my beak but I felt faster than I ever had.

'Your turn, son,' Mickey said, turning to Dave. 'Let's see what that wing can do.'

Dave scoffed. 'I don't need all this training, Dad. I'm a racing pigeon, remember?'

'But you haven't really flown with that wing,' Gary said.

'That's true,' Mickey said. 'Even the greatest racing pigeons need practice.'

'OK,' Dave grumbled. 'I'll have a practice after my nap.'

'No.' Mickey stood firm, blocking the route back to Dave's bed. 'Practice first, then nap.'

Dave stared at his dad and I recognised the stubborn glare in his eyes. 'Nap first, then practice.'

'Practice then nap,' Mickey squawked back.

'Nap then nap,' Dave cawed louder.

'Practice!'

'Nap!'

Jet growled, scaring both Dave and Mickey into silence.

'He started it,' Dave said, pointing at his dad.

'STOP,' Jet howled. 'Everyone freeze!'

The front door rattled as a key twisted in the lock.

'Who's that?' I panicked. In among the piles of dog food and pet toys strewn across the floor, Dave stood motionless, still pointing at his dad. Mickey was leaning forward on one foot, his other claw up high. Jet wasn't blinking and for some reason Gary was balancing three tiny hula hoops around his waist.

'It's the Vet Man's son,' Gary squeaked. 'If we stay veeeery silent, he may not notice us.'

'That'll never work!' I kept as still as possible anyway.

A Human stepped into Pawsville, the bell above the door sounding his arrival. He was looking at his phone and talking to another Human whose face was trapped on the screen as he walked right past us.

'Why is he here?' I cooed as quietly as I could.

'He's here to top up our food bowls,' Gary replied in the tiniest of voices. 'He'll leave straight after.'

The Human carried on chattering to the phone screen while he set down food bowls in the back room. One for Fluffle. One for Cricket-Ball Face. Two bowls of birdseed for me and Dave and a carrot for Gary.

Gary was right. The Human was so hypnotised by the screen, he hadn't noticed us gathered in the reception area.

He just had to refill Jet's kibble and the Human would be gone.

As the final bowl of food was set down on the floor by Jet's dog bed, the Human turned around and came back towards us.

'Hold your positions,' Mickey whistled softly.

Out of the corner of my eye, I could see Dave's head tremble. He'd spotted something.

In front of him were crumbs from last night's biscuit banquet.

I squeezed my eyes shut and tried to send him a message with my mind: don't move, Dave.

The Human was now standing right next to me. The cuffs of his jeans rustled against my bottom.

I held my breath.

Just then, a Dave-shaped shadow moved and I saw my friend change position and peck at the crumbs.

'Hold on a second,' came the booming voice of the Human. 'What's this?'

Nobody moved.

Dave held still, mid-peck.

The Human peered at the phone screen and wiped a scuff of dirt off with the hem of his shirt. 'That's better.'

He strode out of the building and locked the door as we collapsed on to the floor in relief.

'That was a close one.' Mickey turned to Dave. 'I'll make you a deal, son. How about if we train, then you can have two jammy biscuits and a nap?'

'There's only one jammy biscuit left,' Dave said, brushing jam and crumbs out of his feathers.

'Come on, Dave,' I said, swooping up into the air. 'Don't you want to try out your wing?'

I saw a familiar smirk spread across his beak. We may not have been the fastest pigeons in the park, especially when there were abandoned bags of chips to eat, but all pigeons loved to fly and there was nothing better than that feeling of freedom as the air rustled through your feathers and you thrust upwards towards the clouds.

'Come on, Dave,' Jet yapped. 'We want to see you fly.'

As the others gathered around my friend and cheered him on, Dave gritted his beak

and pushed up off the floor. I followed after, staying close by him. He beamed at me as we hovered higher and higher and his new wing clicked up and down. His feet launched off the floor and were soon dangling high over his dad's head.

'QUICKER! HIGHER! FASTER!' Mickey screamed at us as we lunged and soared and leapt and circled.

We got quicker and higher and lungier and worked until our feathers were drenched with sweat. I barely noticed when the sky turned from light to dark.

'YOU CAN DO IT,' Mickey yelled as we cheered Dave, who jumped further and faster, flapping harder and harder before finally catching me as we circled the ceiling, late in the evening.

'It's good to have you home, Dad,' Dave said, collapsing in a happy heap once the training was over. Jet pushed a plate of dinner over to him and Dave chowed down as he chattered happily with Gary and the others.

'What will you do if Dave doesn't win?' I mouthed to his dad. 'You're Mickey Lightning, the legendary racing pigeon.

You've never been on the losing team before.'

'You're right, my boy,' Mickey said. 'And I don't intend to start joining the losing side now.'

Dave! You're back! Have you been eating biscuits for two whole chapters?

Have I missed anything?

Nothing you need to worry about, Dave.

8
To the Pylon on the Hill and Back

It's Race Day, readers!
I hope you have your Dave Pigeon
foam wings and Dave Pigeon baseball
caps and Dave Pigeon bobbleheads on.
I hope you're blowing your Dave Pigeon
vuvuzelas feather-splittingly loud in
the face of all the pirate parrots
because you are now going to hear
about the race of the year.
And I'm in it.

'Is everybirdy ready?'

Dave nodded and flicked out his new wing as Jet, Fluffle, Gary and Cricket-Ball Face chanted the words 'Team Pawsville! Team Pawsville!' over and over and over again.

'Where's Mickey?' I asked.

'Dad will be here,' Dave said. 'Don't worry, Skipper.'

We were gathered outside Pawsville Vets, waiting for Opprobrious Vastanavius the Parrot and his cronies from Dazzle. It was early. There were no Humans about apart from the Man who was driving a street cleaner down the road while his ears were plugged with headphones.

Last night Opprobrious Vastanavius the

Parrot's white cockatoo sidekick had turned up and told us to be ready for an early morning start.

'The race is fifty Human miles long. Twenty-five miles to the pylon on the hill and twenty-five miles back,' he crowed at us from outside the window. 'Prepare to lose, pigeon.'

Mickey had gone before we woke up. Last night I thought I had seen him exchange a strange look with the cockatoo, but I shoved the niggling doubt to the back of my mind to focus on helping my best friend. But as the minutes ticked on that morning, I grew more and more worried. What if he had lost his sense of direction and was heading right and right and right, all the way around the world again?

A crowd of birds started to gather on a telephone wire. One bird flew across the crowd, offering snacks of popcorn and bread crusts from the bin. Crumbs rained down on my head as I paced the pavement underneath, watching Dave practise star jumps and hopscotch.

'Yoo hoo!'

The familiar twinkly call of our Human Lady's next-door neighbour's pet canary rang over my head.

'Tinkles? What are you doing here?'

The yellow ball of feathers landed on the pavement. She brushed down her plumage as she greeted me. 'I'm here to watch Dave lose to the pirate parrot.'

Tinkles had never been much of a friend.

'There they are!'

We followed Jet's gaze up to the sky. She started to yelp and chase her tail as a flock of birds came into sight. Opprobrious Vastanavius the Parrot was in the lead, followed by the fluffy white cockatoo and the two yellow and green budgerigars we met three days ago.

Behind them was another bird. A grey pigeon.

It was Mickey.

'What's Dad doing with Opprobrious Vastanavius the Parrot?' Dave asked, confused.

I had no idea what Mickey was up to but I could see Dave panicking. 'Don't worry,' I told my best friend. 'You've trained hard. You can do this.'

Dave bowed his head as Fluffle, Cricket-Ball Face and Gary formed a circle around him and squeaked his name loudly: 'DAVE, DAVE, DAVE!'

I was furious. How could Mickey let Dave down again?

Opprobrious Vastanavius the Parrot

landed to a roar of cheers from the growing crowd. The budgerigars were prancing around, linking their wings and whistling louder than ever:

Opprobrious Vastanavius will vanquish the pigeon
Because he's a hero and Dave's a wijjin.
And we'll feast tonight on pigeon pie
And Dave will be the first to . . .

'That's enough,' Jet roared at the birds.

what's a wijjin?

I have no idea. Those budgies are the worst at coming up with rhyming shanties.

Mickey crowded in close to Opprobrious Vastanavius the Parrot. I stormed towards him, ready to give him a beakful about not being there for Dave earlier that morning.

'I wouldn't bother talking to him if I were you,' the parrot's sidekick cockatoo said, pushing me back. He pointed at Mickey, who was deep in conversation with the red parrot. 'He's on our side now.'

How could Mickey do this?

Opprobrious Vastanavius the Parrot swooped towards Dave. He fanned out his huge bright wings and called us over.

I took a step towards Mickey, who hung his head and refused to look at me or Dave, but the cockatoo blocked me again. As a mob of birds covered the streets, I saw Mickey being dragged back by the cockatoo, further away from Dave. How could Mickey break his Pigeon's Promise?

Opprobrious Vastanavius the Parrot hopped up on to the cement step by the lamppost.

'Today', he bellowed, 'is the day we decide whether parrots are better than pigeons. I shall race that scurvy pigeon.' He pointed at Dave, tossing his head up away from us as though he'd smelt something bad. 'And I shall defeat him.'

The crowd squawked and shrieked.

Dave stormed over to the step and jumped up, knocking the parrot off with his bottom. 'Not if I defeat you first,' he shouted in Opprobrious Vastanavius the Parrot's face.

Cheers and barks rose from Pawsville Vets as more animals and pets gathered around Jet, Gary and the rest to cheer on Dave. We didn't need Mickey when we had friends like this.

I flew over to Dave and hugged him. 'You can do this.'

'I know,' he said, grinning at me.

'CONTENDERS TO THE STARTING LINE,' a loud voice boomed across the street.

Dave puffed out his chest and followed

Opprobrious Vastanavius the Parrot to the middle of the road. This was it. All of Dave's training came down to this one moment.

A crowd of birds circled Dave and Opprobrious Vastanavius the Parrot, hooting and howling for the race to start, as a budgerigar counted back from ten.

'Nine ... eight ... seven ...'

Feathered bodies shoved and pushed, parting me from my friend.

'Dave—' I called out but a flock of birds closed in, blocking my view.

Dave was on his own.

'Four ... three ... two ...'

The budgie let out a final high-pitched whistle and Dave and the parrot shot up into the sky to the roars of the crowd.

'FLY!'

'COME ON, DAVE!'

Jet howled and Gary scratched at his ball, cheering Dave on. I took off after my friend. Dave sailed through the air, chasing Opprobrious Vastanavius the Parrot as we got to Dazzle.

Dave was flying. He looked strong. What's more, it looked like there might be a chance he could actually win this race.

Arooooooo

9

The First Mile of the Race

It turns out racing is pretty much birds flying and not doing much else but here's what happened.

After one mile Dave was cruising through the air, following closely after Opprobrious Vastanavius the Parrot, who was ahead by about ten beaks.

10
The Tenth Mile of the Race

Opprobrious Vastanavius the Parrot was still ahead by about ten beaks.

11
The Twentieth Mile
of the Race

Opprobrious Vastanavius the Parrot was still ahead by about ten beaks.

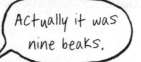

Actually it was nine beaks.

Opprobrious Vastanavius the Parrot was ahead by nine beaks.

Sorry, I got that wrong. It was about ten beaks.

Opprobrious Vastanavius the Parrot was still ahead by about ten beaks.

12
The Twenty-fifth Mile of the Race

Opprobrious Vastanavius the Parrot and Dave looped around the pylon on the hill and started to soar back towards Pawsville Vets.

(Oh and Opprobrious Vastanavius the Parrot was ahead by about ten beaks.)

13

The Thirtieth
Mile of the Race

You guessed it. Opprobrious Vastanavius
the Parrot was still ahead by about ten
beaks.

I've just made up a pirate shanty.

Let's hear it.

Some biscuits are round and some of them are not
And some of them are long and some of them are not
But the worst biscuits arrrrre the ones filled with snot.

That's what I meant. I made up a song about biscuits.

That's not a shanty. That's a song about biscuits.

14
The Fortieth Mile of the Race

Opprobrious Vastanavius the Parrot was ahead. But now by ten and a half beaks.

15
The Forty-fifth Mile of the Race

Opprobrious Vastanavius the Parrot was still ahead but now it was by eleven beaks.

Dave was dropping behind. Fast.

Twelve beaks.

Fifteen beaks.

Nineteen beaks.

'I. Can't. Do. This,' Dave panted as he flapped hard, his new wing clicking and snapping as it struggled to flap quicker.

He dropped behind by five more beaks. And then five more.

As Opprobrious Vastanavius the Parrot became a smaller and smaller dot on the horizon, I knew I had to do something.

'Don't give up, Dave,' I squawked. 'I'll be back soon.'

There was only one bird who could help Dave now: his dad.

I fell behind and searched the flock for Mickey. There he was, bringing up the rear. I blasted through the throng of birds, aiming straight for him.

'Dave needs help,' I said, pulling up alongside Mickey.

'I can see that,' Mickey said.

'What were you doing this morning?' I asked. 'I saw you.'

'Saw me where?'

'With him,' I screeched. 'With Opprobrious Vastanavius the Parrot.'

'It's not what you think,' Mickey shrieked back.

'What were you doing with that parrot when you should have been with Dave?'

'I was trying to talk Opprobrious out of the race.'

'What?'

'I knew Dave had to rest his wing and I didn't want that parrot to hurt my son.'

'You weren't switching sides?' I asked.

'Never.' Mickey grinned. 'I always pick

the winning team.'

'Why didn't you come back and see Dave off?'

'Opprobrious got his crew to lock me in Pawsville,' Mickey cried. 'Everybody had left to follow the race and I was all alone. I had to find the keys, fly up to the lock, peck it open with the keys and then use them to wedge the door open so I could get out.'

'Why does no one ever use the dog flap?!'

Mickey paused. 'That's actually a really good idea.'

'We don't have time for this now.' Up ahead, I could see Dave had fallen behind by fourteen more beaks. 'Dave needs us.'

'Get in my slipstream, Skipper,' Mickey ordered. 'I'm going to get us to him.'

Mickey's slipstream smelt of cabbage and pigeon poo-farts. (You know the ones you do when you aren't sure if you need a poo or a fart so you do a little one and check what comes out.) It might've smelt bad but Mickey still had his racing talent. We soared towards my best friend, who was now sinking lower and lower in the sky.

'Dad?'

'We're here, son.'

'I thought you weren't coming,' Dave said as he gasped for air.

'Of course I was,' Mickey said. 'I'm so proud of you.'

We looked forward and saw Opprobrious Vastanavius the Parrot far ahead. He was now a colourful dot, piercing perfect holes in the clouds as he darted towards the end of the race.

'Full throttle on the feathers, son,' Mickey ordered Dave. 'You can do this.'

16
The Final Mile

'By Hamster Paws!' Jet howled, shocked. 'I think Dave might win this.'

My heart banged away at a million miles an hour. Up ahead both Opprobrious Vastanavius the Parrot and Dave were racing straight for Pawsville. Mickey was squawking encouragement to Dave, who seemed to have found a new surge of wing-power.

Dave had closed the distance between him and the parrot to just eight beaks.

Five beaks.

Four beaks.

Thousands of birds and pets now lined the streets screeching and crowing for both racers.

Opprobrious Vastanavius the Parrot looked back over his shoulder. As he realised Dave was right behind I could see the parrot panic for the first time. He slowed down for a millisecond as Dave rose up beside him.

And then he kicked him.

'Dave!' I screeched.

Dave veered off course and his new wing caught the TV aerial on a nearby house. The harness stretched as its stitches popped out one by one. Dave dangled from the metal, shrieking for help.

'HELP!'

I flew hard, dropping
towards my friend. As I
pulled up close, the harness ripped against the
metal and Dave plunged towards the ground.

'HELP!'

I dived at him and clutched at his head with
my feet. As my claws gripped his fuzzy head
feathers, I slowed, flapping us both down to the
ground, where Jet met us.

'Oh, Dave,' Jet said.
'You almost did it.'

'It's not over,'
Dave said, through
gritted beak.

148

He pulled off the last of the shredded feathers on the harness and started running towards Pawsville. Up ahead Opprobrious Vastanavius the Parrot hadn't yet made it to the finish line. The crowd, having seen the parrot's crafty move in the sky, now cheered for one name and one name alone: DAVE.

'COME ON, DAVE,' I screamed, my throat hurting from cheering for my friend.

Dave was almost at Pawsville. As he mounted the kerb, ready to hit the finish line, a dark shadow of a bird swooped over him and crossed the line first.

Opprobrious Vastanavius the Parrot had won.

Dave crossed the line a moment after.

He dropped to the pavement. His broken prosthetic wing and strands of leather harness now hung featherless, dangling off his body. He let out a tiny coo of 'need biscuits urgently' before closing his eyes and rolling on to his tummy.

Opprobrious Vastanavius the Parrot peacocked across the street and back again, punching the air with fisted wings.

That's when I heard it.

'Dave! Dave! Dave! Dave!'

The crowd was not cheering for the winner. They were cheering for Dave.

'Dave!' I said, shoving my friend. 'Listen!'

'Dave! Dave! Dave! Dave!'

He sat up.

'Dave, they're cheering for you,' I said, pulling him up to his feet.

'But I lost.'

'You might not have won the race, son,' Mickey said, holding Dave up at his side. 'But listen to the crowd. You're their winner.'

Opprobrious Vastanavius the Parrot screeched at the crowd. 'Why are you

cheering for the pigeon? I won! Not him!
Parrots are the best.'

The crowd turned on him, booing as he
and his shipmates backed away.

'You're a cheat, Opprobrious Vastanavius
the Parrot!' Mickey roared. The entire
crowd gasped as Dave's dad revealed what
we'd witnessed in the air. 'My son is the

true winner here. We all saw you kick him out of the sky. You'd better leave now and never return to Pawsville Vets ever again.'

Opprobrious Vastanavius the Parrot snarled at Mickey. 'You pigeons are all the same. You're all fools.' He spat hard at the floor near Mickey's feet. 'I won't forget how you betrayed me and my crew, Mickey Lightning,' he hooted. He took off into the sky with the cockatoo and the budgerigars and we watched them fly away until they disappeared above the clouds.

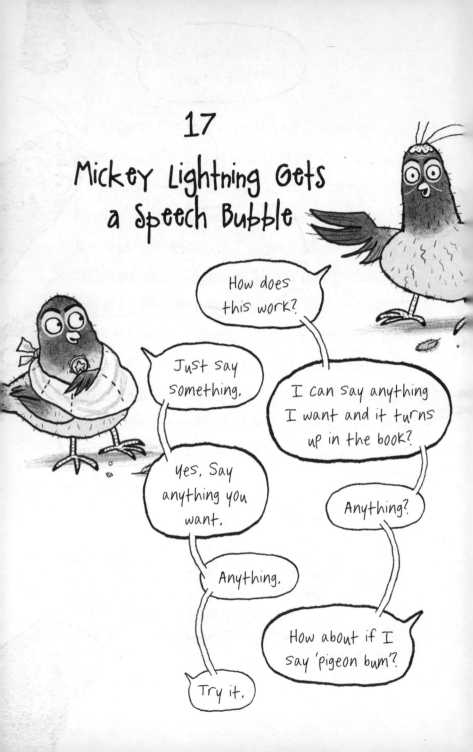

155

Before we left Pawsville, Dave was measured up for a new wing. His prosthetic one had been wrecked during the race and it would be a while before the Vet Man could fix him up with another. But we didn't care. Our Human Lady had come back for us. It had been fun at Pawsville but I was feeling homesick without my Human Lady snuggles and my typewriter.

'Dave! Skipper!' the Human Lady called out as she came through to pick us up. She scooped us into a huge hug and nuzzled the top of our heads with her own.

She then dropped us into the oversized pockets on either side of her raincoat and we discovered we each had a pocket full of jammy biscuits. My favourites.

As the Humans discussed Dave's new wing, Jet, Gary, Fluffle and Cricket-Ball Face waved us off. They watched from the window as we climbed back into the box on the Human Lady's bike. I couldn't help but feel grateful that our time at Pawsville was up and we had our own pigeontastic home to return to.

'I can't wait to be back in our shed and tuck into the secret stash of biscuits,' Dave cooed happily on the ride home.

'I've missed my typewriter,' I agreed. 'Wait. What secret stash?'

'Never mind, Skipper,' Dave said. 'I think we're home.'

As the bike pulled up at the Human Lady's home, the familiar smell of lawn and brick building came flooding up through my nostrils.

We'd invited Mickey to come and stay with us and when he heard about our shed, he leapt at the chance to be in a Human home again even if it was only for a short while. He ooohed and ahhhed over our nest among the paint-tin lids and wonky shelves but he admitted he wanted to find his Human Owner. He'd been away for too long.

But there was something else that put him off staying with us. Something that wasn't quite right at the Human Lady's house. It wasn't the garden. The lawn looked as lawny as ever. And it wasn't the patio. Those paving stones looked as pavy and stony as they always had.

But something had changed since we'd been away.

It was the back door of the house.

There, as it had always been, was Mean Cat's cat flap.

But now, alongside it, sat another cat flap.

There were two cat flaps.

For two cats.

Maybe leaving Pawsville wasn't as pigeontastic as I thought.

Mickey Lightning's Guide to Success

Have you got a school test coming up? Or maybe it's Sports Day? Or maybe you need a wee but your little sister has been in the bathroom doing a poo for the last hour . . . Whatever the challenge, here's Mickey Lightning's Guide to Success to help you win at everything.

Always start your day with these pigeontastic exercises and you will be off to a flying start:

Put your left foot forward
Now put your right foot forward
Now stick your bottom out
And give it a shake.

Stick your left wing up
Now your right wing
And blow a raspberry out of your mouth (or
your bottom if you prefer)

Finally, look in the mirror and tell yourself: I am going to be the best pigeon I can be because Mickey Lightning told me so.

MALPAS

More Terrible Jokes from Jet That Didn't Make It into the Book

(They are terrible. You shouldn't read them. I mean, seriously, they are really awful. Just stop reading. I mean it. Stop reading.)

What do you call a chicken with an egg on his head?
Egg head.

Knock knock.
Who's there?
Sandwich.
Sandwich who?
Sandwich who who.

What do you call a sausage with an egg on its head?
Another egg head.

What do you call a pencil with an egg on its head?
A pencil with an egg on it.

What looks like a frog and smells like a frog?
A toad.